SAFE HANDS

Poems & Short Stories

JESSICA CARELOCK

ISBN: 978-1-943258-68-0
Carelock. Jessica.
Safe Hands

Edited by: Amy Ashby

Published by Warren Publishing

Charlotte, NC
www.warrenpublishing.net
Printed in the United States

Art by Jesse Covington

Dedicated to my mother, for knowing what I was meant to do before I did.

CONTENTS

ACKNOWLEDGMENTS

ELLOW WRITER-FRIENDS are one of the biggest blessings in a writer's life, and the support, encouragement, and advice they provide is vital to the creative process. For that, Elliott, Laura, Lizzie, and Eva, I thank you. Thank you for jumping on board this crazy train with both feet and looking over manuscripts countless times. Thank you for in-depth discussions about word choice, painstaking analysis of the tiniest of details, and treading the balance between blunt honesty and compassionate criticism so beautifully. Most of all, thank you for believing in my ability far more than I did.

To my mother, Sandy, my brothers, James and Paul, and my very best friend, Cayla, thank you for supporting my dreams no matter where they take me. Thank you for pushing me to be better, for encouraging me when I was hesitant, and for reassuring me when I doubted myself. The four of you are foundational pillars in my support system, and without you, my life would not be nearly as full.

Finally, to Jesse, thank you for your art and for loving me so well. You are a continuous fountain of comfort, validation, and inspiration, and I appreciate you for everything you are.

SAFE HANDS

THERE ARE DEFINING MOMENTS in every person's life: moments that will build up or destroy, moments that determine who they're going to be. Sometimes these moments are only noticeable to that person; sometimes they are witnessed by others. Mine was both of these: a series of moments I experienced alone, until they culminated into one huge moment that ended the life I knew.

LEAH

My father is on trial for four counts of child abuse and two counts of child neglect. I sit in the witness stand staring at my knees and picking at a hole in the edge of my skirt that my mother didn't see when she hastily ironed it this morning. I feel my father's eyes on me, but I refuse to look up. I know he will have placed his cuffed hands on the table in front of him. To anyone else it will look like an effort to sit comfortably, but I know it is his subtle reminder that I did this. It is my fault that this sharply dressed man, well-known in our community for his volunteer work and successful surgery practice, is sitting here like a criminal.

The thing most people notice first about my father is his charm. His cornflower blue eyes are surrounded with laugh lines and he has a way of smiling that makes you want to tell him every secret you've ever thought about having. People know he's drawing them in, but somehow he makes them powerless to prevent it. My lawyer says that's going to be the hardest thing for the jurors to overlook during this trial, especially if his lawyer puts him on the stand, which she probably will. I asked my lawyer if we could just blindfold the jurors. He said, 'no.'

My lawyer is a mean-looking man, but he's actually pretty nice. His name is Joe Watts, which is a guy-next-door kind of name. He told me that I could call him Joe unless we were in the court room. Here I have to call him Mr. Watts.

"Could you please tell the court your name?"

No sound comes out of my mouth when I try to respond, so I clear my throat and try again. My voice wobbles but I can't stop it. "Leah Claire Walker." There are so many eyes on me. I can feel the sweat dripping down my spine.

Mr. Watts smiles at me encouragingly. His tone is gentle when he responds. "Leah, could you please tell the court your story?"

I take a deep breath. "My father wasn't always a bad man."

"Daddy!"

"Hey, Pumpkin!" he laughed, picking me up and twirling me around with one arm and shutting the door with the other in one smooth motion. "Where's your mom and brother?"

Isaac came toddling around the corner, bumping clumsily into my father's knees. My mother soon followed, wiping some flour on her apron, and scooped Isaac up in her arms before she pecked my father on the cheek.

"How was work?"

Dad sighed and put me down. Shrugging out of his coat, he ran a hand over his face. "Do you remember the four-year-old girl I told you about last week? I couldn't save her," he said.

"Oh Charles, I'm so sorry."

Waving away her sympathy, he looked down at me and Isaac. "Who wants to go outside and play some baseball?" He looked at my mom again. "I'll keep them out of the way while you finish cooking whatever you've got smelling so nice."

Mom chuckled. "It's molten lava cake." Mom's molten lava cake was one of the greatest things in existence. When you cut it open, chocolate icing oozed everywhere. It was surprise cake!

"Mmmm, my favorite!" he said.

"Mine too, Daddy, mine too!" I chimed in.

He grinned down at me. "I know Pumpkin, yours too."

"So it sounds like you and your father were close?"

I shoot a furtive glance at my father. His eyes are boring into mine, and sure enough his hands are sitting primly on the table in front of him. I quickly return my gaze to my shaking knees. "He taught me how to throw a baseball and how to play basketball. Sometimes he let me put his hair in pigtails when he got off work and Mom wasn't home. He said it was important that I be a girl but know how to hold my own. I think Dad used to love me, once."

"Objection. Creating prejudicial bias."

I startle. This is the first thing my father's lawyer has said since her opening statement the day before. I send a panicked look to Joe.

"Sustained. Counselor, please redirect your client," says the judge.

JOE

This poor child. I watch her fidget on the stand and once again question the wisdom of letting her give her testimony. She alternates between looking at me and her father — between seeking reassurance and expressing apprehension. I've been doing this for about ten years now and this is what I despise about my job. Every day I am confronted with children who have experienced horrific things that nobody, *especially* a child, should ever experience. The worst part is that it's often extraordinarily difficult to get a conviction. Most of the cases rest primarily on the testimony of the child, and so often it's just not enough. I don't tell anyone that, of course.

About eight months ago, Leah walked into my office wearing a neatly pressed dress, tights, and perfectly shined shoes with her dark brown hair pulled back into a tidy ponytail; absolutely nothing like the dirty, scuffed-up children I usually work with.

"Are you Mr. Watts?"

"I am. Who are you?"

"My name is Leah. I need your help." She pulled out a beat-up coffee can and placed it on my desk. "I heard you help lock up bad people. I know this isn't enough, but I can get the rest for you. It might take my whole life, but I promise I'll get it to you."

I glanced into the can. There was a crumpled up five dollar bill, a few ones, and some change: all in all about fifteen dollars. Leah stared at me expectantly. She was a scrawny girl, all knees and elbows, and every inch of skin possible was covered by clothing. I leaned back in my chair. "How old are you, Leah?"

She glanced down at her shoes. "I just turned twelve."

"Does anyone know you're here?"

"No. I told my mom I was going to the library and took a bus."

"Well Leah, you know I'm not supposed to talk to you without a parent or guardian present."

Leah took a deep breath and looked me in the eye. "What do I do when the bad person *is* my parent?"

LEAH

November 1st, 2003 was the first time my father hit me. I remember because it was Isaac's third birthday. I was six years old. He came home from work and dropped his briefcase on the table by the door in the foyer.

"Daddy!"

Instead of smiling and picking me up like he usually did, he brushed me off. "Not now, Pumpkin."

Walking into the kitchen, he went straight to the fridge and pulled out two beer bottles without a word to my mother.

"Charles? Is everything okay?"

"I met with a mother today…" he responded after a long pause, one hand on the handle of the refrigerator, his eyes downcast. His voice wavered and tapered off. My mother waited for him to continue. "I had to tell her I couldn't get all of the cancer, there was too much, it was just too far gone. Her son is going to die and I couldn't stop it." He looked in the direction of my mother, but his eyes were vacant. He was looking through her. I hid behind my mother. "Do you know what it's like, looking into the eyes of a mother and telling her that her child is going to die? Knowing there's nothing you can do?"

He walked into the living room without another word. I heard the soft sigh of his sinking into the overstuffed armchair by the fire and then the television crackled to life. My mother's hushed voice came from behind me.

"Leah-bug? Will you take Daddy some crackers? He's had a hard day and he's probably hungry."

I took the crackers from her hand and edged into the living room. Shadows danced across the wall, the light from the television playing like a ghost against Daddy's face. As I sidled up to his chair, he opened the second bottle. He drinks quickly when he's upset.

"Daddy? Mommy sent you some crackers. She said you might be hungry."

He took the crackers from my outstretched hand and put his hand on my head. My mother walked in, tugging on her jacket, and grabbed the keys from the bowl by the door.

"Isaac and I are going to run to the store. I'm going to grab some eggs for Isaac's birthday cake and pick up some oregano for the spaghetti. Are you guys going to be alright here?"

"We'll be fine," Daddy responded.

"Okay, we'll be back soon!"

Isaac tottered toward the door, looking like a marshmallow in his big winter coat. My mom took his hand and helped him to the door and out into the blustering cold that smelled of snow.

"Leah, get me another beer."

I didn't think he should have any more, but I got him one anyway. As I handed it to him, I tried to climb up into his lap. He shoved me roughly and I landed hard against the coffee table.

"Oh, Pumpkin, I'm sorry. Come here. No, no, don't cry. I didn't mean to push you so hard. I just had a rough day. I'm sorry."

He held me against his shoulder as he opened the beer bottle. The stench of beer washed over me and I buried my face in his neck. He smelled of the cologne my mother had bought him last Christmas, a combination of cedar and the leather of his armchair. As I breathed in his familiar scent, I felt relieved. This was my daddy. He didn't mean to hurt me. I slid off his lap to the discarded puzzle Isaac and I had left on the floor earlier that day. As I struggled to make sense of the mother tiger and her cubs, I chattered away to my father about my day.

"I got to be the line leader at school today. John almost got to but Ms. Watkins picked me instead. Then at lunch we had tater tots. After lunch we got thirty whole extra minutes of recess and then—"

"Leah, get me another beer."

"Oh. Okay."

I hurried to the kitchen and took a bottle from the fridge, then rushed back to the living room. Rounding the corner, I tripped over the upturned corner of the rug. The beer bottle

fell from my hand, and I watched in horror as it toppled end over end before smashing onto the stone hearth of the fireplace. Dad was on his feet and standing over me before I could blink.

"You stupid, clumsy girl!"

I barely saw his hand lash toward me before my face whipped to the right, knocking me backwards into the edge of hearth. I lifted my hand to my stinging cheek and scooted backwards away from him. He'd hit me. My daddy had actually hit me.

"I'm sorry, I'm sorry, I'm so sorry."

"Clean it up!"

I ran to the kitchen to get a towel and a broom. Daddy's eyes were filled with regret when I walked back into the room. I sopped up the liquid and carefully swept up the broken glass.

"Daddy? I'm really sorry," I whispered. "It was an accident."

He walked over to where I crouched by the pile of broken glass. "You know I didn't mean to hit you, don't you, Pumpkin?"

I looked at him with watery eyes and didn't say anything, terrified that I might say something wrong.

"We don't need to tell Mommy about this, it was all an accident. You understand that, right?"

"Yes, Daddy."

The door jangled as Mom and Isaac walked back in. Mom was laughing. "We're back!" she sang out. She stopped when she saw the broken beer bottle. "What happened here?"

"I dropped the bottle on my way back to my chair. I may have had one too many!" he laughed, and his grip tightened on my shoulder.

I shook my hair down across my face and didn't say a word.

RUTH

God have mercy on this poor, sweet little child. From the jury box I can see her shaking all over. She's sitting on a stack of phone books so she can see over the witness stand. She's just a little sprite of a girl, not unlike my granddaughter. She opens her mouth to tell us her name, but she can't speak. Bless her heart, she must be terrified. Who can blame the poor thing, so many people staring at her? When she does speak, I'm surprised. This isn't the voice of a twelve-year-old girl. Her face is blank as she begins to tell us what happened to her, and there is no emotion in her voice. The things she must have seen, must have experienced, to make her this way.

I look toward her father, Dr. Charles Walker. Everyone has heard of him, of course. You can't live in this town and not know that name. He's always in the newspapers for something, volunteering at homeless shelters, expanding his surgery practice and the like. I tell you, I was absolutely shocked when I heard about the crime he had been accused of. Nobody wanted to believe such a dreadful thing about such a good man.

His hands are resting on the table in front of him. I stare at them and try to fathom if those hands that have healed so many people could turn around and hurt someone as innocent as little Leah. That wife of his, nobody ever hears anything about her. Could she be upset about his fame? Maybe she wishes he were home more.

He turns his gaze to me, as if he can feel me staring at him, and flashes me a sad smile. Oh, this poor man. What a dreadful thing to be accused of. He reminds me of my husband when he was a younger man, with those eyes and that smile, and the way he's so involved helping others. How could someone like that do something like this?

LEAH

"Leah, can you tell the court how often your father hit you?" Joe asks.

"It was just that one time for a while. He said he was very sorry. I thought that if I was on my very best behavior, everything would go back to the way it was before. It worked for a while I guess, but—"

"Objection. Avoiding the question."

"Your honor, this is the way my client feels like it makes sense to answer the question," Joe explains. "If the court could just listen for a moment, we'll hear the answer."

"Overruled," the judge says, turning a kind face toward me. "Leah, please continue."

"It worked for a little while," I continue, "but he couldn't save all the children. He tried very hard, people don't realize how hard it is for him to not be able to save them all. There was one time, about a year later, where he lost several all in one week. That was a bad week. That was the next time he hit me."

I was sitting on the floor in the living room, reading a story to Isaac. Mom was reorganizing the garage, so it was my job to keep Isaac entertained and out of the way until Dad got home.

"Richard wanted a dog," I read. "Any kind of dog would do. But his mom said a dog was tooooooo much trouble, so she bought him a lion. It was a nice lion. It was almost like a dog, but—"

"A lion isn't like a dog!"

"I know, that's the point!"

"Well why would she buy him a lion then?"

"Isaac, you can't keep asking questions if you want me to keep reading. The point is to *listen.*"

We heard the keys jam in the door, and after a couple faulty attempts to unlock it, my dad opened it. He stalked into the living room, muttering to himself. I took one glance as his face—his eyes tight and every muscle tense—and knew today would be a bad day. Isaac snatched the book out of my hands before running over to my father. I watched in horror as my father glared down at him.

"Daddy, why did Richard's mommy buy him a lion when he wanted a dog? Lions aren't like dogs. Dogs are better. They let you play with them and feed them and pet them and you can't do that to lions. His mommy should have given him a dog instead because—" I thrust my hand over Isaac's mouth and dragged him out of the room under my father's scowl.

"You can't just attack him like that! Can't you see he's mad? You're going to get in trouble!"

"Sorry, Leah. I'll be better, promise!"

Isaac scampered down the hall and I returned to the living room. Dad was sitting in his armchair staring blankly at the Western playing on the television. Clint Eastwood ran across the screen, firing bullets at all the bad guys, but Dad wasn't watching. There was a 'w' etched into his forehead that I longed to smooth out, and his eyes were wide open without seeing anything. I reached a tentative hand out toward his elbow, but quickly withdrew when his empty gaze turned toward me.

"What do you want?" he bit out.

I turned my face to the floor. "I just wanted to ask how your day was."

"Speak up! You know I hate it when you mumble!" he barked.

I took a step back and repeated, "How was your day?"

"I lost three patients today, how the hell do you think it was?"

"I'm sorry, Daddy. Can I bring you something to drink?"

"Get me a beer."

I scurried out of the room into the kitchen, flinging open the fridge, only to find that there were no beers. I could feel my heart beating in my ears, and my palms started sweating. Saying a quick prayer, I opened the pantry door and saw an unopened box tucked away in the corner. After refilling the fridge, I opened a bottle and returned to the living room. I handed the bottle to my father and tentatively watched him take a sip. It barely had time to pass his lips before he was spitting it back out.

"Where the hell did you get this? I asked for beer, not warm cow piss! All the things I do for you and this damn family, and this is the shit I get back?"

I flinched at his harsh words. Lurching out of his chair, he grabbed the back of my head. His fingers tightened into my hair and he dragged me from the living room. My eyes blurring from the tension of his grip on my hair, I stumbled along unseeingly as we moved toward the kitchen. I felt my knees slam into the tiled floor as he shoved me roughly away from him and flung open the cabinet door.

"Do you see this?" he demanded, pulling a glass out of the cabinet and placing it on the counter. He moved to the freezer and pulled out the tub of ice. "And this?" He slammed the tub down beside the glass and angrily tossed some cubes into it. "*This* is what I expect when I ask you for a damn drink, you stupid girl! I don't know why I bother with you, you useless piece of shit!"

Breathlessly, I stammered, "I'm sorry, Daddy. I'm so sorry. We didn't have any cold ones, I'm sorry—"

"I don't want to hear your excuses! Get out of my sight!"

I fled the room as tears etched trails down my cheeks.

The defense lawyer stands in front of me, arms crossed. Joe couldn't prepare me for this part, but he did show me a picture of her so I would know what to expect. I think if I met her on the street, I wouldn't know she was a lawyer because her face is smiling and her blonde hair looks like my pediatrician's. But standing here in front of me is a woman who looks like a mama bear pulled out of hibernation too early, and that makes her the scariest woman I have ever seen.

"You claim your father has been abusing you since you were six years old, is that correct?"

"Yes, ma'am."

"And you also say you and your mother were very close?"

"Yes, ma'am. My mama is my best friend."

"Then why did you never tell your mother?"

I pause. "I didn't want anything bad to happen to her. Isaac needed her, I needed her. And she loves Daddy, more than she loves anybody. As long as I didn't say anything, nothing would happen to anyone else."

"It's been a while since you were six years old. Do you remember much about being six?"

I think for a moment. "I don't guess so. I started first grade that year and my teacher was nice. And I remember what happened with Daddy."

"Do you remember what presents you got for your birthday that year?"

"No, but—"

"Do you remember your school assignments from first grade?"

My throat starts to feel like it's closing up. I wipe my sweaty palms on my skirt as she stalks toward the stand.

"Well, no, but—"

"What about a play date with a friend from your class? Or a neighbor? Can you remember that?"

"No, but—"

She lifts her chin, challenging me. "If you can't remember any of those things, why should we believe that you can remember the exact day your father hit you?"

I start to panic. Joe told me to be specific. He said that would help. Why isn't it helping? I cast a gaze around the room, desperate for reassurance, but none comes. Joe sits silently at his table, and the uncomfortable look on his face tells me there's nothing he can do.

ROSE

Some days I hate myself and what I do. As I watch Leah unravel on the witness stand, I think to myself that today is one of those days. Based on the case file, there is no doubt in my mind that this child was abused by the man I am defending, but I don't get to choose the cases I defend.

"Because it was Isaac's birthday, I remember because of Isaac's birthday!" she shouts, and the desperation for somebody to believe her is almost tangible. She seems to fold in on herself, wrapping her arms tightly around her abdomen and searching wildly around the room for someone to help her.

"Leah, did you ever finish that penguin puzzle you were working on with Isaac that day?"

She looks up mistrustfully at the sudden shift in subject.

"…Yes?"

"You did finish the penguin puzzle?"

"Yes," she says with building confidence.

I cock my head to one side. "That's interesting, considering you told the court it was a tiger puzzle."

Her eyes grow wide and she falls mute. I turn to the jury. "Ladies and gentlemen of the jury, Leah is a child, and her memory has obviously been clouded. We can't be expected to believe a serious accusation if she contradicts the details she testifies as fact. No further questions."

I settle myself back at my table and try to ignore the feeling of self-hatred filling my heart. It's not my job to believe my client, it's my job to defend him and that's exactly what I'm doing.

LEAH

"She made me look like an idiot in front of everyone!" I say to Joe as soon as we have a break. "Nobody is going to believe me now!"

"Calm down, take a deep breath." His tone is calming as he takes a seat in the chair beside mine. "She's just doing her job. The jury hasn't made their decision yet, this could still go either way."

"Go either way?" I fidget anxiously in my chair. "Why would they believe me? You heard her ask me those questions I couldn't answer. You said to be specific and I tried, I really tried, but I didn't do it right and—"

Joe grabs my arms and looks me in the eye. "Leah, do you trust me?"

"Leah, do you trust me?"

Daddy's eyes were desperate. He was kneeling in front of me, holding my arms rigid against my body. I examined his eyes, looking for something, but they were empty of anything but wild desperation.

"Yes, Daddy."

"Okay. So, you know it was an accident? I've just been a little off, but I'm getting better. I'm seeing someone who can help me, and I'm getting better. I just need you to trust me."

I couldn't tell what I was supposed to do. He looked unkempt; his hair was oily and stuck to the sides of his face, his shirt was untucked, and his eyes were red and swollen.

"Okay, Daddy," I say.

"Come here, Pumpkin." He wrapped his arms around me tightly. "I love you more than anything. Things will be different now, I promise."

Maybe this time really would be different. Maybe he'd keep his promise.

"Leah? Leah? I said, 'Do you trust me?'" Joe repeats himself and I'm back in the court house.

I scan Joe's face, looking for a sign that everything will be okay. "Yes, Joe. I trust you."

"Good. Our strongest witness is yet to come, okay? I need you to trust him—and me. We're going to get through this together. Now take a deep breath and let's get back in there."

With that he turns around and follows the bailiff back into the courtroom. I take a few more deep breaths to calm myself before trailing after him. When I sit back down beside Joe, he reaches over and gently squeezes my shoulder. "We can do this."

I nod and look up to the empty bench where the judge sits. The door beside it opens and the bailiff walks in.

"All rise for the honorable Judge Samuel Cardozo."

SAMUEL

They think I called this break for them, but it was mostly for me. The tension in that room was stifling. I shouldn't even be on this case in the first place: I don't usually work domestics. The wife of the judge assigned to it went into labor, so the rest of us took all his cases…and I drew the short straw because I'm the most recent transfer from lawyer to judge. Nobody wants the child abuse case. So much of it is he-said, she-said, plus the emotionality attached to it is draining. I sink into the chair behind my desk, close my eyes, and gently massage my temples. I imagine the knot of tension that sits there, which I can feel but cannot quite touch, and think back to the meeting I had with the prosecutor and defense attorney earlier this week.

Rose Maculler is a chameleon: whoever her clients need, that's who she becomes. Teenager caught with drugs? Maculler is a warrior against absent parents leaving a child to grow up without love and direction. Old man perving on kids on the playground? She is an understanding friend who knows he's just a lonely man, deserted by his kids in his old age and craving human interaction, not creepy. She is equal parts kind and ruthless, benevolent and malicious. That's probably why she has a high success rate, and definitely why Charles Walker chose her to defend him.

When I read the name of the defendant on the case file, my first reaction was that sinking feeling you get in your stomach when you miss a step on the stairs. I don't know whether he abused his daughter or not, but I can almost guarantee he won't be convicted unless the prosecutor has some hard evidence for it. In addition to it being difficult to convict someone for child abuse in the first place, Dr. Walker being such a prominent member of society will make the jury even less likely to convict him, even though it's his own daughter. His status in the community also makes this a high-profile case, which in turn means it's closely monitored by the media. Right this second there are reporters and camera men from seven different news agencies around the country sitting outside my courtroom, waiting to see how this case ends.

When I met with Maculler and Watts this week, Mr. Watts was trying to get an agreement from Maculler to have Dr. Walker observe the trial on a monitor in my chambers rather than being physically present during Leah's testimony.

"Your Honor, this is absolutely ridiculous. Why should we change the precedent for this case?" Maculler asked. She was perched on the edge of her chair, leaning into her words, as if that would make them stronger.

"She's a twelve-year-old girl." Watts was calmer, and sat relaxed in his chair. "It would be inhumane to force her to sit there with the man who *abused* her less than fifteen feet away. She has been traumatized by this man—"

"You mean, 'man who *allegedly* abused her;' he hasn't been convicted of anything. Your Honor, the Confrontation Clause of the sixth amendment clearly states that the accused has the right to confront his accuser. Taking my client out of the courtroom denies that right and is an obvious violation of our Bill of Rights, the very rights this country is founded on, the rights—"

Watts leaned forward. "Violation of rights? If you want to talk about violated rights, you should look at my client. She has the right to feel safe and secure, a right that has clearly been violated and will continue to be if she is forced to look into the eyes of the man who was supposed to love her, protect her, and—"

I held up a hand. "Counselors, please." I waited for their full attention before continuing. "Ms. Maculler, I am well aware of what the sixth amendment states, but thank you for being so kind as to point it out. Mr. Watts, as it stands, there is no law to condone what you are requesting. If we made an exception for your client now, we would have to do the same for every other person who makes an accusation against another. I appreciate the situation this places your client in, but I can't make an allowance for her because I have to also protect the rights of the accused. He has the right to be in the presence of his accuser, and I can't take away that right to accommodate your client."

As I anticipated, this was not the response Watts wanted, but it was the one he expected to get. "Thank you for your time, Your Honor," he said before turning toward Maculler. "I will see you in court."

With that, he picked up his file notes and left the room, leaving Maculler staring after him. She glanced back at me after the door shut and it was like looking at a different person. All her fight left with Watts and what was left was a shadow of what was before. Her mouth opened and shut without a word, and then she exited the room, abandoning me to be alone with my thoughts.

PETER

"Dr. Rudge, could you please state your name and profession for the court?" Joe asks.

"Certainly," I say. "My name is Dr. Peter Rudge and I am a psychiatrist specializing in mental disorders, specifically narcissistic personality disorder, bipolar disorder, and depression."

We rehearsed this testimony for six hours yesterday, so it is not a surprise when he plays the devil's advocate. "Aren't all psychiatrists specialists in mental disorders?"

"No. Some specialize in mood disorders, autism, or substance abuse. We all have an understanding of mental disorders as a whole, but my research and education goes deeper than basic psychiatric learning."

"Prior to today, have you seen the defendant?" asks Joe.

"Yes, I met with him to do a court-ordered psychiatric evaluation a few weeks ago."

"Based on that evaluation, what is your professional opinion of his mental state?"

"I believe that Dr. Walker suffers from bipolar disorder with elements of narcissistic personality disorder."

Joe flashes me a smile and glances over to the jury. "My medical vocabulary isn't as strong as it should be, I'm afraid." As he predicted, several jury members smile and chuckle. He turns his glance back to me. As a psychiatrist for the court, this is not the first testimony I've given. However, Joe seems to be more adept at playing to the jury than many of the lawyers I've worked with. "Would you mind explaining a bit about those mental disorders?"

"Of course not. Bipolar disorder is defined as a mental condition affecting your mood, causing you to experience moments of extreme elation closely followed by moments of extreme depression," I explain. "Somebody who is bipolar will face these mood swings in rapid succession, sometimes multiple times throughout the day. Narcissistic personality disorder is a mental disorder that causes a person to have a magnified sense of their own importance, a deep-seated need for admiration, and an absence of empathy for others. However, someone who suffers from this disorder will have very low self-esteem that will exacerbate the slightest criticism."

"How might these mental disorders manifest themselves in someone like the defendant?" Joe asks.

"Dr. Walker is a highly-regarded member of the community. As a result, there is a lot of pressure on him from a multitude of places: work, home, in the community. This pressure would feed Dr. Walker's need for attention, but at the same time if he loses a patient, which he would see as a personal failure, everybody sees it. For someone with narcissistic personality disorder to have their failures broadcasted for the world would be detrimental to their already fragile sense of self-esteem, and could result in them lashing out violently."

"Objection. Speculation."

I look up to the judge. "I'll allow it," he says.

At his nod, I continue. "Dr. Walker also suffers from bipolar disorder. The impact that these failures have on him from a narcissistic angle could very well be triggers for a dramatic mood shift. Those who suffer from bipolar disorder can be easily triggered into a mood shift by children, because children often lack the awareness to understand when their actions cause annoyance. They have a lot of energy, which can be over-stimulating for someone who is bipolar."

Joe leans back against his table. "Wow, it must be very difficult for someone to live like that. Are there options for treatment?"

I nod. "There are. There are different types of therapies, as well as medication that can be taken to regulate mood."

"What was Dr. Walker doing to control his mental state?"

"He was seeking a therapist to work through his narcissistic personality disorder and taking medication to control his bipolar disorder. However, he did neglect to take his medication periodically, which would explain his actions toward Leah."

Maculler is on her feet immediately. *"Objection.* That is an inflammatory response operating under the suspicion that my client is guilty."

Judge Cardozo looks down at me. "Dr. Rudge, I'm going to have to disallow that remark and have it removed from the record."

Joe told me that would happen, but it doesn't matter. The seed has already been planted. I hope that man rots in prison.

SARAH

"Isaac, please! Can't you just sit still and be quiet for *five minutes?*" I've had it with this child. Isaac won't stop asking questions. He's being difficult today, and my nerves are stretched thin enough as it is. I grab his arms. "Isaac, buddy, I'm very stressed right now and I really need you to calm down for a little while. Will you please go read quietly in your room?"

He nodded and ran off. I reach for the abandoned dust cloth on the coffee table and returned to my stress cleaning. I don't know how this happened. After all, I'm with my children every single day; how did I miss it? *Because you didn't want to see it.* The voice in the back of my head is right, of course. I missed it because I refused to see it. Does that make me a bad mom? Or does it make me a good wife?

I told the court that I couldn't find a babysitter for Isaac through this fiasco, which is technically true, but I didn't really look, either. I don't think I could sit in that court room and choose between my baby girl and my husband. Can anyone really choose? When I married Charles, I vowed to love him forever. The two of us became one person. And then we created a person. We created another human, a symbol of the love we have for each other. I will never forget the look on his face when he held Leah for the first time. The wonder that this little person was ours, the awe at her perfect little fingers and toes! She was so tiny in his arms. He was the perfect father; always the first to scoop her up when she fell off her bike, the one who taught her how to defend herself from bullies. He even let her paint his toenails after she had done her own and mine. And oh, how that little girl loved her daddy. She was his shadow. When he was home, she was two steps behind him everywhere he went. There was so much love there, I don't understand how it changed.

LEAH

The jury has been deliberating for the last three hours. Joe says that means at least one person doesn't agree with the rest. I don't know what to do. I've been driving Joe up the wall by asking every five minutes if they're ready yet, and no matter how hard I try, I can't stop shaking. It's hard to swallow and my chest hurts from how hard my heart is beating. The air feels heavy and small, even though I know it can't be. It's like I'm the only one who knows the world is ending, but nobody will listen when I try to warn them.

At that moment the door opens and the bailiff comes out to tell us the jury is ready to make their decision. Joe and I follow him back into the courtroom and take our seats. When the courtroom settles, all eyes turn toward the jury. Some faces look sad, but I can't tell what's going to happen from their faces. Judge Cardozo looks to the foreman of the jury.

"Mr. Foreman, has the jury reached a verdict?"

"We have, Your Honor."

"What say you?"

I hold my breath and reach for Joe's hand.

"We, the jury, find the defendant, Dr. Charles Walker, not guilty on four counts of child abuse and two counts of child negligence due to insufficient evidence to support a conviction."

I choke on the breath I was holding. *Not guilty.* I look at Joe. "What happens now?" I whisper.

He looks at me with pity. "There's nothing else I can do. I'm sorry, but he's going to be released to go home now."

I wake up in a dark room with Joe holding a cold cloth to my head. He tells me I've just had a panic attack.

"I'm sorry, Leah. I did the best I could. I want you to take these." He pushes a tape recorder and a notebook into my hands. "I wrote my information down in the notebook," he says. "You record everything that happens to you and Isaac. If it happens again, you document it. We'll get him next time, Leah. I promise."

I nod, but I know there won't be a next time. Next time I won't make it.

THE FRIENDSHIP OF
A BROKEN HEART

My heart has rejoiced and broken for you
a thousand and one times.

It has celebrated your successes and your joys,

It has grieved your failures and your sorrow.

It has soared on the wings of promise, and born the weight
of pain.

My heart has carried your fear, your anguish, your anger.

It has felt your loss, your doubt, your insecurities just as
strongly as it has my own.

But sometimes I wonder,

Has your heart ever broken for me?

SMEARED LIPSTICK

*V*ERONICA WAS LATE AGAIN. She always seemed to be late now. Steven had just turned eight and was at that difficult stage where he wanted more independence than he was capable of and disliked the idea of his sister, Violet, being able to boss him around. Veronica sighed and reached into the backseat of her beat-up Honda to grab the bag of makeup she had purchased on her way to the party and hastily applied it. It had been so long since she'd needed makeup that all of hers was out of date. She felt like an awkward school girl as she hesitated by Katherine's front door, her hand hovering over the doorknob.

After several false starts, Veronica finally opened the door and walked in, one hand clutching her casserole dish, the other anxiously tugging on the hem of the short red dress Katherine had forced her to wear. Her eyes scanned above the crowd for her friend. She took in the table laden with food and the swirling mass of people in the dimly lit room, her whole countenance shifting to relief when she found Katherine standing by the kitchen. She made her way through the throng of people, hastily murmuring apologies to those she bumped into, and greeted Katherine with a quick hug.

"Hey, Kat. I brought a lasagna but by the looks of that table out there you won't be needing it. Sorry I'm late."

Katherine placed the dish on the counter, then stood back and assessed Veronica's outfit, taking in the dress hem pulled down and the neckline pulled up farther than intended, the slightly smeared lipstick, and the blonde hair one gentle whisper away from leaving its hasty constraints and dissolving into a chaotic mass of curls. "Definitely not having this," she muttered as she adjusted the dress and fixed Veronica's lipstick before pulling out her hair clip, releasing the curls to tumble softly to her shoulders.

"Much better!" Katherine declared, taking Veronica's hand and dragging her through the kitchen to the living room. "Okay, his name is Ryan, just turned forty, never married. He's a lawyer, loves kids, volunteers with the Red Cross, and listens to Bach when he studies his cases. Got it? Good."

Katherine tugged her over to a man with a friendly smile who towered over Veronica's already tall frame. His wavy auburn hair that had begun to grey around the temples and the laugh lines around his eyes were the only indications of his age.

"Ryan! This is my friend Veronica, the one I was telling you about!" With that pronouncement, Katherine dropped Veronica's hand and disappeared into the crowd, leaving the two very much alone.

"Um... Hi, Ryan," Veronica stammered, once again fidgeting with the hem of her dress.

"Hello," Ryan responded with an easy smile. "It's very nice to finally meet you. Katherine has been telling me about you for quite a while. She says you're a surgeon?"

Ryan could not have picked a better conversation starter; there was nothing Veronica loved more than her work. The tension in her shoulders eased and the knot of anxiety in her stomach started to unwind as she began telling him about the hospital where she worked, her colleagues, and some of her patients. Ryan was the perfect listener, asking questions at all the right places and laughing when appropriate.

"He did *what?*" Ryan asked incredulously.

Veronica laughed. "He woke up! Right in the middle of the surgery. I'm up to my elbows in his intestines and he's asking me if he's dead."

"What did you do?"

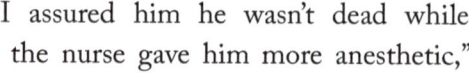

"I assured him he wasn't dead while the nurse gave him more anesthetic," Veronica said, smiling. "He went right back to sleep and didn't remember it after. I tell you what, it's disconcerting having a person talk to you while you're holding his liver."

Gradually their conversation shifted to his work, and later on to more personal things. She talked about her kids and he told her about his sister.

"Steven is eight and thinks he's quite the little man," she said. "And his sister is no better. She's fifteen now and not old enough to know what she wants, but old enough to know it's not what I want from her."

Ryan chuckled. "I understand that. I don't have any kids myself, but my sister is ten years younger than me and I looked out for her a lot when our dad died. She was quite the handful when she hit that age. She turned to sports though, and that seemed to help her change her focus."

Veronica nodded in agreement and found herself opening up to Ryan more than she had to any other man since the death of her husband six years previously.

"I've been at a loss with them since Nick died. Steven wanted to know why Daddy wasn't coming home for two years after the accident. Violet understood, but pushed everyone away." Veronica paused. "He was on his way to meet his mistress. Can you believe that? Isn't that ironic, him dying in a car accident on his way to meet another woman? Violet knew before I did; she was Violet's volleyball coach. She told me about the affair, but I didn't have a chance to confront him before he died." She let out a bitter bark of laughter. "And the best part? That woman had the audacity to show up at the funeral claiming she had no idea he was married."

Suddenly Katherine appeared and anxiously yanked Veronica off the sofa where she and Ryan were now sitting. "V, you have to go. Like now. Right now," she declared, hauling Veronica toward the door. They were nearly outside before Veronica could even process what had happened.

Ryan called out after them. "Wait, Katherine! I want Veronica to meet my sister. She just got here a few minutes ago. I think they will really get along!"

At that moment, the front door opened and in breezed a tall, willowy brunette. Intelligent sapphire eyes above a sharp nose and perfect scarlet lips surveyed the room. The color drained from Veronica's face.

IT WAS THE WAY

It was the way the left side of your mouth lifted a little higher than the right when you smiled that made me realize I was in love with you.

Not just that I loved you, but that I was *in* love with you.

It was the way you walked slightly in front of me in crowds so I didn't get pushed around,

The gentle way you linked our arms so I was never left behind.

It was the thousand different ways you said my name, but especially when you were exasperated and it sounded like a sigh and a kiss all at once.

It was the way you said you could see the one-armed gorilla doing a handstand in the clouds that I saw, even though I knew you didn't.

It was the way you smiled and rolled your eyes at my jokes but secretly laughed when nobody else was around.

It was the way you looped your arms around my waist and gently dropped a kiss on the top of my head while I cooked dinner,

The way you briefly rested your hand on the small of my back when you walked around me.

It was all the little things that tied our hearts together, and the moment you severed those knots was the moment I knew I had lost you forever.

SUPER HERO

Dear Ian,

*Y*OU'VE BEEN GONE for twelve whole hours now. Mom says your plane should be landing in Afghanistan soon. She says I should write you letters while you're gone. I will try to write you letters, but I'm eleven now so I might be busy. I have homework and friends and stuff. I hope you make friends while you're gone! Middle school is hard. Mom doesn't know but I already peeked in your room to see if you left anything behind. I took your favorite hoodie. I'll take care of it until you come home. Mom and Dad say you won't be home for a while. Does that mean I can have your room? Write me a letter back as soon as you get this. I'm timing the mail man.

Love,
Julia

Dear Jules,

I've arrived safely now! Your letter followed me to base and got here about a week after I did. I know you'll be busy in middle school so I'll forgive you if you're slack with letters! Thank you for taking care of my hoodie! I was worried that I left it behind, but I feel better now knowing it's in safe hands. I'll be home by the time you're twelve, so you stay out of my room!

I have made a friend. His name is Ivan and he's from Nebraska. He's got a little sister about your age!

Don't be too harsh on the mail man, he has to wait for a truck to take this letter to the airport, the pilot to take it to the States, another truck to take it to the post office, and *then* the mail man can bring it to you. It's not his fault it will take a while!

Love,
Dan

Dear Ian,

It took a whole month before I got your letter back. I guess that makes sense though if it had to go through everything you said it did. Did my letter get as beat up in the mail as yours did? Yours looked like it got chewed on by a dog. Are there any dogs in Afghanistan? Do you like it there? Mom and Dad say I should pray for you extra because it's dangerous where you are. I told them you were invincible, just like Wolverine. Mom got a little bit mad at you. She said you shouldn't have let me watch that movie. I didn't mean to get you in trouble. Don't worry though, she still loves you.

She misses you a lot. I found her crying on your bed today. She was holding your pillow. I didn't know what to do so I just left. Dad stays away a lot but I think he misses you too. We're having Chinese food today. I don't know why though, you're the only one who really likes it and you aren't here to eat it. I asked Mom if I could mail you some but she said it would be bad before it got there.

I'm glad you made a friend. What's his sister's name? Is she pretty? Would we be friends?

At first it was fun being the only kid here but now it's not. You've been gone long enough. I think you should come home now.

Love,
Julia

Dear Julia,

A month or so between letters sounds about right! It might be longer for the next few because I will be doing some extra missions and I won't be able to write. Your letter was nice and neat! Mine was probably beat up because I had to carry it in my pocket for a few days while I waited on the truck. I've been working hard out here. It's quite hot, even at night, especially when we have to wear so much protective gear.

I appreciate your prayers! Mom and Dad are right; it is pretty dangerous over here. But don't you worry, I can handle whatever happens. You're right, I am like Wolverine! It's okay that you told Mom we watched that movie together. She won't be mad for long.

I would have loved some Chinese! We don't get any of that over here. Mom is right though, it would be bad by the time it got here. Give her an extra big hug from me. Will you tell Dad it would be nice to hear from him? I hope to be able to come home by this time next year!

Ivan's sister's name is Megan. I don't know if she's pretty or not, but I'm sure the two of you would get along.

Love,
Ian

Dear Ian,

Happy birthday! Turning twenty-two means you're getting old now. I ate a cupcake with a candle on it for you today. I got my own birthday party this year and I hated it. I miss sharing a party. So far twelve sucks.

I dropped one of my favorite earrings down the sink today. I asked Dad if he could get it out, but he just grunted at me. He smelled like that whiskey bottle you brought home that one time and told me to keep a secret. He and Mom have been fighting a lot this week. They don't think I know. He always leaves and Mom sits in their room and cries.

I got an 'A' on my history and geography test today. I got all the bonus points because I knew where Afghanistan, Iraq, and Iran are. I'm glad you made a friend over there.

You said you would be here by my birthday. I wish you were.

Love,
Jules

Dear Julia,

Happy late birthday to you too! I missed our shared birthday party too. I'm sorry I couldn't be there. My leave request got declined because they needed me to run another mission with Ivan. I wish I was there to help you and Mom. When Dad smells like that, stay away from him. He loves you but sometimes people do things they don't mean.

Good job on your test! I'm so incredibly proud of you! I'm glad you're doing better than I did in school. Keep up the good work!

Love,
Ian

Dear Ian,

I started high school today. I wore your hoodie because it fits a little better now. I was the smallest in my class again. I wish I could grow a foot in a month like you did in high school. Homeroom was okay. I have Ms. Green and she seems nice, just like you said she would be. She said I look just like you. Everybody said that. "It's the eyes," they said. "You have the same blue eyes." I sat close enough to the front that my teachers would think I was trying, but close enough to the back that nobody would call me a teacher's pet.

Mom was hovering when I got home, just like you said she would be in one of your other letters. She made me chocolate chip cookies just like she did for you. It wasn't the same though because you aren't here. She asked me how school was and I said it was fine. Then she asked how my classes were and I said they were fine too. She asked about the bus ride home and the food at lunch and I said they were all fine. She laughed and said I sounded just like you.

Dad hasn't been around much.

How's Ivan?

I miss you.

Come home soon?

Love always,
Jules

Dear Jules,

I miss you too! See, I told you your first day wouldn't be so bad. High school is daunting at first, but it's really not so bad once you get there. Ms. Green is sweet, I know you'll love her. She was my homeroom teacher for three years, so I would know! Don't tell Mom, but Ms. Green will look the other way if you're a little bit late or you decide to eat chocolate in her classroom. She'll let you chew gum too. Who else do you have? Avoid Mr. Acronaro at all costs. He's a creep. You should also try out for some sports teams. You're great at volleyball, so why don't you try out for that? The volleyball coach is tough, but she's good.

Give Mom a hug from me and try to put up with her hovering. She worries about you, you know. Make sure she knows how much I love her! I hope to get accepted for leave soon and I'll come home ASAP. I'll let you have the sand in my boots as a souvenir!

Write back soon, your letters make my day. Maybe you can send me some of those chocolate chip cookies and we can eat them at the same time. Then it'll be almost like I'm there.

It'll be a while before my next letter because I'm being sent to a new place. I'll be going into enemy territory, so it'll be more dangerous. Don't worry though, everything will be fine! You'll always be my favorite munchkin! I love you!

Love,
Lau

Dear Ian,

I hope you're okay! I've been watching the news lately and they're all talking about the soldiers in Afghanistan.

I had my first date today. I haven't told anybody about it but Mom. His name is Noah and he's a really nice guy. We went out for pizza after school. He was a real gentleman. He opened my door and paid for the food, and was just really nice. He even brought me roses! I didn't know guys did that type of thing anymore. I told him all about you. I can't wait for you to meet him! I know you'll like each other.

You didn't say anything about Ivan in your last letter. I hope you guys are alright!

Can't wait to talk to you!

Love,
Your favorite munchkin

Dear Ian,

I know you won't get this for a while but I wanted you to know that I'm graduating early. They're going to let me finish as a sophomore because I've taken a ton of extra courses and they've all been AP. That means I'm done by this time next year! I don't have a whole lot to tell you about. You remember Noah, the guy I was seeing? Well, we're still together. He told me that he loved me last week. I think we're getting pretty serious. I'm kind of crazy about him.

Hope to hear from you soon!

I love you to the moon and back!

Love,
Jules

Dear Ian,

I graduated today. Really wish you could have been there. I had to give a speech because I was Valedictorian. I half expected you to come in halfway through, you know, like they always do in those "Soldiers Come Home" videos? Mom and Noah both brought me bouquets, one yellow lilies and the other red roses. Dad didn't even bother showing up.

You're going to have a stack of these when you get back from your mission!

Love you!

Love,
Julia

Dear Ian,

I'm engaged! It was so romantic how Noah asked me. We had been talking about getting a dog, so we went to the shelter to pick out a puppy. I found the most adorable Husky German Shepherd mix and when Noah gave me the collar to put on her, there was a ring on it! He told me that he wanted to spend the rest of his life making me happy. We've set the date for April 16th of next year.

Happy birthday to you!

Love,
Jules

Dear Ian,

It's wedding day! Grandpa is walking me down the aisle. I haven't spoken to Dad in three years now and since you're not here, Grandpa said he would step up. The bridesmaids are all in purple halter-neck dresses with white rose bouquets, and the groomsmen are wearing grey suits with purple ties. My dress is gorgeous! It's strapless with a corset back and lots of beads! My bouquet is beautifully made up of white roses and purple lilies. You don't like flowers, but I'm sure even you would admit that it's beautiful. Mom has been a blubbering mess all day, but she's excited for me. The only thing that could make this day better is if you were here.

Love,
Julia

Dear Ian,

It's been a while. Noah and I have two kids now, twins. One boy and one girl. We named the boy Ian Michael, after you, and the girl is Isabel Michelle. Ironically enough they were born on April 15th. They're two years old now and love hearing stories. Their favorite is about Uncle Ian, the brave soldier. They call you a super hero. I heard them telling their teacher all about how Uncle Ian went away to Afghanistan to beat up all the bad guys. They always look at your picture when they go to Nanny's house, and every night they sleep with the quilts I made them out of your sweatshirt.

I miss you.

Love always,
Jules

YOU'LL REMEMBER

You came to me guarded and broken, scared
to believe, scared to trust, scared to love.

You came to me totally unprepared for how completely I
would fix myself into your life.

I mended your broken spirit with words of comfort, brick
by brick, I slowly took apart the walls you had so carefully
built around yourself.

I opened your heart to love, made you believe in your
future, and etched my name firmly into your soul,

So firmly that when you cut your hair, you'll remember
how I liked it sort of short, just long enough to run my
fingers through.

When you look at grass or see moss on the trees, you'll
remember the exact color of my eyes.

When you go outside and feel the sun on your face or hear
the whisper of the wind, you'll remember our walks to the
ocean when I kissed your cheeks and whispered in your ear
the way they did.

When you get in your car to drive, you'll see me laughing
in the shotgun seat.

When you turn on the radio, you'll remember dancing
in the kitchen at two in the morning.

When you go to all your favorite places,
you'll remember taking me there,

Because when I leave, I'll destroy you in
the most beautiful way.

ABOUT THE AUTHOR

*J*ESSICA'S love of language was born when she was three years old and spent most of her time demanding one more story. From there, it blossomed as she read every book she could get her hands on and began writing her own stories and poetry. While working toward her BA in English and Creative Writing at Plymouth University, Jessica discovered a whole new world of literature and after graduating, began her career as an editor.